MW01029765
Elder Tree
CAPITOL
St. John's Wort
Meadow
Clara & Melissa's home

The Herbalist of Yarrow

A fairy tale of plant wisdom

The Herbalist of Yarrow

A fairy tale of plant wisdom

  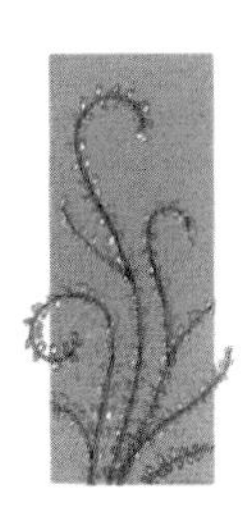 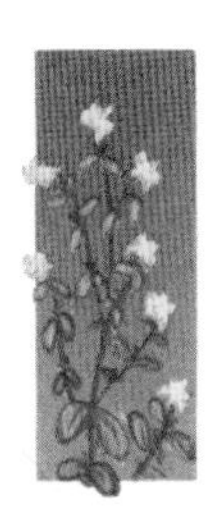 

Written and Created by Shatoiya de la Tour
Illustrated by Pamela Becker

TZEDAKAH PUBLICATIONS
Sacramento, California

Manufactured in China

For information, address
Tzedakah Publications
P.O. Box 221097
Sacramento, CA 95822

Cover and text design by
Lisa Bacchini, Karen Phillips, and Mary Burroughs.
Illustrations by Pamela Becker.

Library of Congress Cataloging-in-Publication Data
De la Tour, Shatoiya, 1954
The herbalist of Yarrow: a fairy tale of plant wisdom / written
and created by Shatoiya de la Tour: illustrated by Pamela Becker.
p. cm.
Summary: A young girl begins to doubt her mother's teachings about the healing power of herbs when the king and his wizards attempt to enforce the use of more powerful medicines. Includes recipes for herbal remedies.
ISBN 0-929999-04-5, $15.95
[1. Fairy tales. 2. Herbs--Fiction.]
I. Becker, Pamela, ill. II. Title.

PZ8.D373He 1994
[Fic]--dc20
94-16072
CIP
AC

FIRST EDITION
10 9 8 7 6 5 4 3 2 1

To those who have had the greatest influence on my herbal path: Rosemary Gladstar, Marina Bokelman, and the students who have been such a blessing to me and to Dry Creek Herb Farm.

To those loved ones who offered endless spiritual support: Barry and Chenue, Bibi, Christine, Kim, Sharon, Aunt Marjorie, Mum, Tani and, most especially, Bubba.

ACKNOWLEDGMENTS

My deepest thanks to all at Tzedakah
—David, Laurie, and Lisa.
Thank you, David, for the encouraging talks under the
pear tree, and the creative hand-holding.
My gratitude to Pamela Becker for her artistic vision
and the talent to back it up. And many thanks to
the designer, Mary Burroughs.
Love to Valerie for her conversion of cut-and-paste
to readable disk and for her extensive care
of Lucy, the wayward dog.

FOREWORD

In my heart, I often remember my first meeting with Shatoiya. It was many years ago. She came to The Herb School, a student full of enthusiasm, zest, and possessed with a great hunger to learn all there is to know about the plants. I'm sure it was her vibrant, alive spirit coupled with an inner courage to live her dreams as well as that flamboyant red hair that endeared her to me forever. I recognized early that this wild, woodland woman had a special affinity for the plants; it's been a delight to watch that interest flower and grow.

When Shatoiya first informed me she was writing a "Tale of Plant Wisdom" for children, I was delighted and knew on the spot it would be wonderful. When the finished manuscript was sent to me to review, I made a cup of tea, found a sunny spot in the garden, and settled down to read with curiosity. Just what would my dear friend and fellow herbalist have to say to children about the wisdom and wonder of plants? How would she find a way to convey to our children these simple earth teachings that seem light years away from the messages they receive daily from our overly exposed, traumatized, TV world?

A few sun-soaked hours later, I emerged fully engrossed from a wise, moving and very powerful story. As meaningful for adults as it is for the children it was written for, *The Herbalist of Yarrow* bears, in the tradition of every true fairy tale, a message quite pertinent and auspicious for our modern world. Woven artfully within the pages of this wise little tale is the story of our current health crisis and the "give away" of our own healing powers.

The true beauty and wisdom of this tale, however, is the gentle imparting of herbal wisdom as it's been passed down through the ages, from generation to generation, from mother to daughter. *The Herbalist of Yarrow* is at work restoring the art of this ancient tradition and passing the teachings along to our children. Oftentimes, I could hear the voices of my own wise herbal elders — my teachers, grandmother Mary, Juliette de Bairacli Levy, Adele Dawson — scattered throughout the pages of this book. And I could hear the words and teachings I shared with Shatoiya in the gardens and woodlands of The Herb School: Honor the plants for their life, thank them for their medicine power, use only what is needed, and always give back to the earth. Shatoiya joyfully carries these earth teachings and weaves them into a wonderful tale that will instruct the children of our future as well as delight the child in all of us.

Rosemary Gladstar
Author of *Herbal Healing for Women*

Not so long ago there was a village called Yarrow. In this village lived a young girl named Melissa.

Melissa was named after a beautiful herb that grew in her mother's garden. She was happy to be named after this plant and liked to sit by it on sunny afternoons. She would rub her hands through it to release its lemony scent. Sometimes she would pick a leaf and chew it. Its flavor reminded her of lemonade. If ever she felt sick, her mother would steep the herb in water to make a hot cup of tea for her. It always made her feel better.

Melissa's mother, who was named Clara, knew how to use the plants because she was the village herbalist. She was responsible for the health of the people who lived in Yarrow. She knew which herbs to use for colds or flus or broken bones, or almost any sickness anyone ever had. Many of her medicines came from her own garden, but she would also gather special plants from the forest surrounding Yarrow.

For the most part, life in Yarrow was peaceful and happy. The villagers were farmers and craftspeople who traded among themselves or with travelers passing through. Four times a year, the villagers would pack up their wares in carts and journey to the Capital, a large city where the King and his armies lived. There, during the cross-quarter festivals, the villagers set up tents and sold their wares to the Capital dwellers. Although most of the children loved the change and the excitement of these journeys, Melissa did not. She was disturbed by all the noise and dust of the city and longed to return to Yarrow.

She especially did not like the soldiers who were loyal to Frederick, the Duke of Allopathy. They were not like the friendly and noble soldiers of the King's guard, who wore brightly colored costumes decorated with braids and plumes. The Duke's soldiers were loud and boastful. They looked mean in their dark tunics and metal breastplates, their faces hidden by helmets.

It was said that the King himself was a good man but that some of his court were wicked. Some, like his cousin the Duke, were hungry for power. Melissa's mother believed this hunger came because they did not allow the earth to feed them.

"They've lost their connection to the earth," Clara would say. "They seek position, gold, and castles to fill themselves up. But they will never be full until they find their peace in Nature."

If ever Clara was unsure about what herb to give a sick person, she would consult her Treasure Book. She called it her Treasure Book, she told Melissa, because it was worth more than all the gold in a pirate's chest. In this very old book were recipes for salves, potions, and other herbal mixtures. This book had been handed down to Clara from her mother, who had received it from her mother. Each generation preserved this treasure of time-honored remedies, and each generation added new remedies of its own discovery. Melissa was always excited when her mother allowed her to take the Treasure Book out and look through it. She knew that one day it would belong to her.

The book smelled old, and some of the pages were brittle with age. Melissa loved to read the old scratchy handwriting and look at the pictures. There were drawings of plants and drawings showing how to make things from them. On pages were pressed flowers dried many years before. What she liked best of all were the little stories that told about people who had been sick and how they became well.

Clara told Melissa, "The best way to learn about the plants is from the plants themselves." She sent Melissa into the garden, meadow, or forest to wait patiently for each herb to reveal itself. Sometimes a fairy or guardian would speak for it. Melissa was used to seeing fairies, brownies, and elves among the plants. She had never seen an angel, though, until the day she decided to visit the angelica plant.

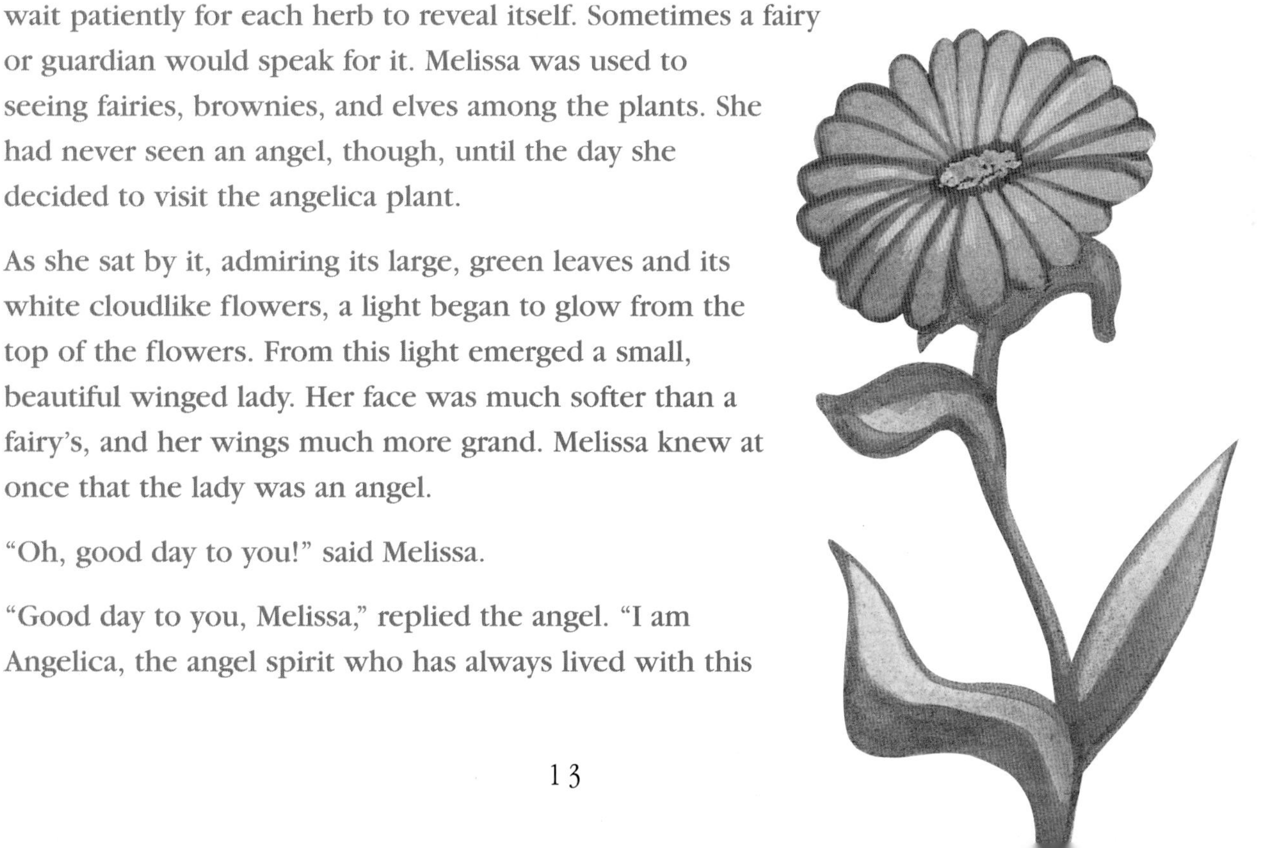

As she sat by it, admiring its large, green leaves and its white cloudlike flowers, a light began to glow from the top of the flowers. From this light emerged a small, beautiful winged lady. Her face was much softer than a fairy's, and her wings much more grand. Melissa knew at once that the lady was an angel.

"Oh, good day to you!" said Melissa.

"Good day to you, Melissa," replied the angel. "I am Angelica, the angel spirit who has always lived with this

plant. That's why it was named after me."

"I've never met an angel before," Melissa said.

Angelica smiled. "All of earth's children have personal angels they can call upon. If you want to make sure your angel stays close by, you can carry a piece of angelica root in your pocket or in a little pouch around your neck. If you wish your angel to come to you in your dreams, place a piece of my root underneath your pillow."

"I think my mother makes medicine from this plant."

"Yes. The root of the angelica is warm and strong. When you are feeling cold and weak in your lungs, my root will help you. A hot tea of angelica root mixed with licorice root tastes good, and if you drink it often, you will soon be up and out the door to play."

"Is there anything else this herb is used for?" asked Melissa.

"Some people gather the larger outside stems of the green plant to make candy. The stems are peeled, boiled, and cut into bite-sized pieces. They are boiled again in honey water, then placed out to dry." The angel smiled at Melissa and said, "The taste is heavenly."

"I will ask Mother if we can try that. Thank you, Angelica. I will think of you whenever I see or use this special herb."

"Blessings to you, my child," said the angel.

The light from the flowers glowed, and when it disappeared, so did the plant spirit of angelica.

Melissa's friend Jon was the blacksmith's son. He, too, was learning a family trade. For his first project, he made an iron rack for Melissa to hang her herbs on to dry them. He also forged iron nails for her to use in making her own medicine cabinet. In return, Melissa made Jon a healing balm. She put herbs in it to cool and soothe the little burns Jon sometimes got from the sparks that flew from his father's forge fire.

Melissa used St. John's wort as the main ingredient in the balm she made for Jon. Because the herb was Jon's namesake, she believed it would have extra healing power for him. She also knew that the plant was especially good for burns because the herb had told her so!

The first time Melissa met St. John's Wort, she saw that he was a hearty fellow. She had gone to her favorite meadow and found him there, standing tall and strong, with his golden head and hands held up to the sun.

"I bring golden, healing energy from the sun down into my body," he told her in his deep voice. "With my roots I bring up earth energy. They mix around in my body to make strong medicine."

"I am thankful for your medicine," said Melissa. "My mother mixed your blossoms with oats when I had chicken pox. After I drank that tea, I felt relaxed and my itching stopped."

"Yes, I'm very good for that sort of thing. But I have other uses as well. Come, pick one of my flowers."

Melissa knelt down and picked one.

"Squeeze it between your fingers," he told her.

As she squeezed the yellow flower, a scarlet juice was released.

"That's the blood of Saint John," he said. "I was named after a holy man who lived long ago. My red juice is a symbol for his red blood, and it has many restorative properties. It can help you heal and take away your pain."

"My mother makes an oil from St. John's wort. Now I know where the red color comes from!"

"An oil made from my blossoms is very good for all kinds of burns. You'll find me useful if you stay too long in the garden without your hat. What does your mother use my oil for?"

"Oh, many things! Whenever I get a bump or a bruise, she puts your oil on right away, and it makes me feel better. Old Hilda from the village gets some from us to rub into her painful joints. When the Mayor pulled his back during the May Day tug-of-war, he said it was the only thing that helped him. The farmers even use it on their horses if they start to limp."

"I'm happy to be of such service," St. John's Wort said,

JON'S BURN SALVE

(See page 75-77 for instructions on making oils and salves.)

In a double boiler heat:
1/2 cup St. John's wort oil
3/4 cup comfrey oil
3/4 cup calendula oil
Add 2-1/2 ounces melted beeswax. Stir well.

Oil should not come to a boil but should be warm enough so that the beeswax blends easily and does not harden.

Remove from the heat. Add 1/2 ounce essential oil of lavender. Stir well and immediately pour into the containers.

Allow the salve to cool completely before putting the lids on the containers.

bowing low.

"We also use your leaves for magic," Melissa continued. "Our ancestors passed knowledge of your protective powers down to us. Every June we pick fresh bundles of you to place around our windows and doors. It is said to keep out evil spirits."

"Well, I don't know if I believe in evil spirits, but I am glad I make you feel safer."

All of a sudden, Melissa felt a strange presence, as if someone were watching her. She turned to see. There, at the edge of the meadow, stood an old man dressed in dark gray. He wore a hooded cloak so his face was barely visible, and he held a tall walking stick. Melissa thought he might be a beggar. Her mother had taught her to be kind to those unfortunate people.

"Come here, child, and speak with me," said the old man.

Melissa bent down and gathered her belongings into her basket. As she did so, she also picked some St. John's wort. She held it tightly in her hand as she approached the stranger. As she got closer, she could see clearly that he was not a beggar. His cloak was made from finely woven cloth. His staff had engraved silver caps on both ends.

"Good day to you, sir," Melissa said as she curtsied.

"Good day, child," said the old man. "I heard you speaking to someone just now, yet I see no one. To whom were you speaking?"

"St. John's Wort, of course," said Melissa.

"You mean the plant?" asked the old man, surprised. "For what purpose does a young lady converse with a green thing?"

"Why, sir, if you listen to them, plants will tell you many things. Mostly I am learning of their healing powers, for I want to be an herbalist."

The old man threw his head back and laughed. "Plants? Healing powers? Hah! Have you not heard, child, of the medicines of the King? His wizards are making healing potions that will put these plants to shame. If people are sick, they can take the King's remedies and be well at once. No one need miss even a single day of work."

"What are these potions made from?" asked Melissa.

The old man tucked his cloak tightly around him. "That," he whispered, "is a secret. But never you mind. The wizards' medicines will soon be spread over the kingdom, and all will know their worth."

"What about the plant medicines? We've been using them for generation upon generation. What will happen to the plants?" Melissa asked.

"Bah! Forget about your plants. Flowers are best used to decorate the hair of fair maidens. Real medicine is made from much stronger ingredients." And with that the old man turned and walked toward the village.

Melissa ran home from the meadow. When she opened the door, she saw her mother preparing vegetables for their evening meal. Melissa hugged her and asked excitedly, "Mother, do you know about the wizards' potions?"

"Yes, dear. Why do you ask?"

"I met an old man near the meadow. He told me the remedies of the wizards were going to be used throughout the kingdom. He said they were better to use than the herbs."

"And what do you think about that?" asked Clara.

Melissa became quiet. She had been so astonished by the old man's words and so anxious to hurry home to tell her mother that she never stopped to think whether his words rang true.

"I don't know," Melissa answered. "You've always told me to listen to the wisdom of my elders, and he did seem like a wise old man. But you've also told me to listen to the teachings of the plants."

"Perhaps both have something to offer," Clara said. "What did this man look like?"

"He frightened me at first. He was dressed all in gray, with a hooded cloak that hid his face in shadows. He carried a beautiful walking stick with silver caps on it."

Clara thought the man Melissa met was indeed a wizard himself. She did not want to tell Melissa, though, unless she was absolutely sure.

HERBAL FOOTBATHS

If the herbs you want to use for your footbath are roots, bark or berries, simmer them covered on the stove for 15 to 20 minutes. Add about a handful to a 2-quart pot. Pour the mixture, herbs and all, into a glass or stainless steel bowl, or plastic tub big enough to fit both your feet. Have a pitcher of cold water nearby, and add cold water until it is cooled just enough to put your feet in. You want it as hot as you can take it. Make sure you are sitting in a comfortable chair or couch. Soak your feet until the water becomes cool.

If you are using leafy herbs and flowers, put them directly into your bowl or tub. Pour boiling water over them.

continued on page 22

HERBAL FOOTBATHS

continued from page 21

Add cool water as above. Let the herbs dance between your toes as you soak in the fragrant waters.

This is a wonderful treat to do with a partner. After your footbaths, sit across from each other on the couch with the other person's feet in your lap. Give each other a gentle foot massage using an appropriate herbal oil.

Some suggested herbs for footbaths: lavender, thyme, roses, ginger, peppermint, rosemary, calendula, scented geraniums, comfrey (leaf or root), lemon balm, sage or eucalyptus.

"Melissa," Clara said kindly, "someday, perhaps soon, you will have to decide for yourself which medicine path you wish to follow. For now, I will tell you what I know of the King's medicine. I have heard," Clara continued, "that in the castle towers of the Capital live the King's wizards. They stay in their cold stone towers day and night, fires burning and pots boiling. They claim to be medicine makers, but I was told that they don't use much of the plants. I don't know what they make their potions from."

"Do the sick people who take these potions get better?" Melissa asked.

"I've heard different stories from the Capital dwellers I have met. Some say yes; some say no. All I know is that when people turn away from the plants that have always been here to feed and heal them, I feel sad." Melissa saw a tear come to Clara's eye as she said, "Plants give us so much, and in return ask only to be remembered. They are part of our connection to the earth. If we lose that, where will we be?"

Melissa thought of her many herb friends in the fields and forests. She recalled seeing them change from seed to sprout to plant to flower to seed again, learning the cycles of life as she watched. She had learned about strength from the deeply dug root herbs and about beauty from her mother's delicate roses. Songs were taught by tree leaves calling through the wind. Melissa vowed never to forget all that the earth had given her.

That night, Clara and Melissa took good-smelling footbaths with rosemary and rose petals. Then they took turns massaging each other's feet with sage oil. They sat across from each other, each holding the other's feet in her lap. As they rubbed and patted each other's feet, they talked together about the garden and the herbs. They spoke of Melissa's school lessons and of the tasks to be done the next day. When it was time for bed, Clara took some lavender branches down from her drying rack and placed them by Melissa's pillow so she would have a deep sleep.

The next day, Melissa's friend Jon did not come to school. She decided to visit him on her way home. As she neared Jon's house, she could hear the clanging of his father's hammer, metal on metal. The blacksmith's shop was behind their house, half of it enclosed, half of it out in the open because of the tremendous heat from the forge fire. Melissa thought it a magical place. Pieces of metal were scattered here and there, waiting to be shaped by Jon's or his father Thor's hand. Jon was older than Melissa and already quite skilled at his family's trade.

Melissa went to the front door and knocked. Hestia, Jon's mother, answered the door.

"Why, Melissa, come in! It's good to see you," said Hestia. "Your mother was just here."

"My mother was here?"

"Yes," Hestia sighed. "Jon is very sick. His chest hurts, and he is coughing. Your mother brought me herbs to make into tea for him. She says he should stay in bed at least two days."

Just then they heard someone talking with Thor outside. Hestia and Melissa walked to the back of the house and peeked through the window. At once Melissa recognized the old man from the meadow. He was dressed in his gray cloak, and its hood still covered his head.

"I am Hemlock," she heard him proudly tell Thor. "I have traveled far from the Capital, and I am in need of your service."

"What might we do for you, sir?" asked Thor.

"The silver tip from my staff has broken and fallen off," the old man explained. "It must be repaired before I travel farther."

Thor admired the silver tip Hemlock handed to him. Then he said, "Such fine work needs a more gentle hand than mine. Unfortunately, my son, who would gladly do this work, is ill."

The old man paused a moment. "Ill, you say? Perhaps I can do something for him."

"I thank you for your concern, sir, but the village healer has already come this morning. She has given him herbs and recommended two days of rest," said Thor.

"Herbs, bah!" Hemlock raised his voice. "Blacksmith, I have with me great medicine from the King's wizards. It can do much more than herbs. If I make your son well again within the hour, will you call it a fair trade for fixing my staff?"

"I don't mean to doubt you, sir, but it seems quite impossible that he would get well so quickly. If you do what you say, though, Jon would gladly mend your staff. It would be worth the work to see him up and around again," said Thor.

Thor and Hemlock went into the house. Hestia and Melissa stood aside to let them pass, then followed the men down the hall to Jon's small room, where Thor spoke to his son. Hemlock stood over Jon. He took a bag out from under his cloak, and from it he took a small pouch. He shook the contents of it into his hand. Out fell little white balls about the size of roly-poly bugs. Hemlock directed Jon to swallow two of them with some water. Jon looked to Thor. When Thor nodded his approval, Jon took the strange medicine.

"Good," Hemlock told Jon. Then he turned to Thor and said, "Let him rest a while. Soon he will be ready to work. I will leave the silver tip and my staff here. I'm sure he will be up to repair it. I shall pick it up in the morning."

"Well, we shall see, sir. Good day to you," said Thor.

"Good day," said Hemlock, and he disappeared down the road.

Melissa knew she had to wait to see what would happen. She offered to straighten up Thor's shop. Then she visited with Hestia. Just when she thought she would give up and go home, Jon emerged from his bedroom, fully dressed and ready to work! He was very excited.

"Mother, Melissa! It's like a miracle! I was lying in bed when all of a sudden I felt a great power running through my body. My chest stopped hurting. I have much energy again and feel strong all over! I'm going to help father right away." He kissed his mother on the cheek and rushed to the forge.

Hestia touched her cheek where Jon had kissed it. “I’ve never seen him like that before!” she smiled. “I guess those old wizards do know a thing or two about making medicine.”

She went to the kitchen and returned with a small package. She handed it to Melissa and said, “Take these herbs back home to your mother. I don’t think we will need them now.”

Melissa quietly took the package and headed home. She felt very confused. She had always believed in her mother and in the herbs. Now she had seen with her own eyes which medicine was more powerful. She was not eager to tell her mother what had happened at Jon’s house.

When Melissa opened the door, Clara asked, “Did you stop to play with someone on your way home?”

“No,” said Melissa softly. “I stopped at Jon’s house. Here,” she handed Clara the package of herbs. She tried not to cry.

“What is in here?” asked Clara.

“Just a bunch of flowers!” Melissa could no longer stop her tears. She ran to her room and sobbed into her pillow.

After a few moments, Clara came into Melissa’s room. She sat down on the bed beside her and stroked Melissa’s hair. Once Melissa calmed down, she sat up in her mother’s arms and told Clara all about what happened with Hemlock and Jon.

"I am not surprised you are upset," Clara soothed. "It is always hard when we start to question the things we believe in. Sometimes it is a test of faith, or it might be a time to rethink our beliefs."

"I saw it," said Melissa. "I saw that the wizards' medicine is more powerful."

"More powerful is not always better. Time will tell. Sometimes just waiting and being patient is the answer. Try to let your thoughts settle. Have faith that the answers you want will come as you need them."

Melissa nodded. Somewhere deep down inside, she knew her mother was right.

"One thing we know for sure," said Clara, "is that herbs taste good. Let's have our dinner now."

Melissa was hungry. They feasted first on salad with spring flowers, then enjoyed the main course of nettle cheese pie. Clara and Melissa shared a teapot full of sleep tea before bedtime. Then they both fell into a deep, restful sleep.

The road Melissa took to school passed by an old elder tree. Melissa always stopped and curtsied to the tree, as her mother had taught her, for Elda-Mor, who lives in the elder tree, is the strongest spirit of the fairy realm.

The very next day, when she curtsied to the elder tree, Melissa heard a voice.

"Good day to you, Melissa."

She looked through the creamy blossoms of the tree. A dark-haired spirit-woman appeared. She wore a crown of dark jewels that reminded Melissa of the rich, dark

elderberries the tree offered in the late summer. Seeing her through the blossoms was like looking through a lovely lace curtain. Although Melissa could not see her clearly, she could tell the spirit-woman was quite beautiful.

"I'm Elda-Mor, queen of the plant spirit realm. I am pleased that you have been taught to honor me and others in the herbal domain. I have decided to share a few of my secrets with you. Put your basket under my branches."

Melissa placed her gathering basket, which she always carried with her, under Elda-Mor's boughs. Falling slowly, as if dancing, the elder blossoms drifted from the tree into her basket until it was full.

"Here is a healing gift, my child," said Elda-Mor. "Whenever there is fever and flu, drinking a tea of my flowers will ease it. Elder blossom tea is helpful for coughs, too. Bathing in my waters will help ease itchy skin and bring relief from measles."

"My mother keeps a bottle of your flower water on her dressing table," said Melissa.

"Washing with it makes your complexion smooth," said Elda-Mor. "My blossoms are often included in beauty creams. My leaves can be blended with comfrey, plantain, nettle, and St. John's wort to create a soothing salve for rashes, bumps, and bruises. But that is not all. My berries, when dark and ripe, make a tasty treat. You can add them to pancakes and muffins. And they make a delicious, healthful jam."

"Elda-Mor, now that I know about the gifts you offer, I will honor you even more."

"Thank you, Melissa. You may let your friends know this: Whoever shall sleep under my branches on a full-moon night will be invited to dance with the fairies.

And also give them this warning: Never pick my flowers, leaves, or berries without first asking my permission, or there will be no healing power in them."

"Yes, I will tell them," Melissa promised. "Thank you, Elda-Mor, for all your gifts." Then she asked shyly, "Elda-Mor, do you know anything about wizards?"

"I've heard of them, yes. But they are of no concern to me, so I have spent little time thinking about them. Why do you ask?"

"Oh, never mind. It's nothing." Melissa curtsied, picked up her basket and headed for school, excited to share her morning's conversation.

Again Jon did not come to school. As soon as the school day ended, Melissa started toward his house. She met her mother on the road.

"Mother! Where are you going?"

"Probably to the same place you are—to Jon's house," said Clara. "Hestia sent word that I was needed."

When they arrived at the house, Hestia greeted them quickly, as she had been anxiously waiting for Clara. She led them down the hall to Jon's room. He lay on the bed, looking very pale.

JON'S COLD AND COUGH TEA

Mix together the following dried ingredients:

1/2 ounce elder flower
1/2 ounce mullein leaf
1/2 ounce lemon balm
1/2 ounce borage
1/2 ounce chamomile
1/4 ounce nettle
1/4 ounce plantain
1/4 ounce red clover

Using 1 teaspoon of the herbal combination for each 1 cup of water, pour boiling water over the herbs. Cover and allow to steep for 15 to 20 minutes. Strain off the liquid. Honey or apple juice may be added for flavor.

General suggested dosage for acute situations:

For children 12 and older, make 1 to 1-1/2 quarts of tea and have them sip it all day long.
For children 7 to 11, 1/2 cup every hour up to 4 cups total daily.
For children 3 to 7, dilute tea by 1/2 with hot water. 1/2 cup every hour.

To use as a respiratory tonic during cold season, make as above, dilute with juice and drink as a beverage daily.

"What has happened here?" asked Clara.

"Well," Hestia said, looking at the floor and wringing her hands. "Yesterday Jon was fine after that strange old man gave him some medicine. You saw him, Melissa. He was full of energy and went right back to work. He worked the rest of the day and worked by lamplight into the night. He stopped only for dinner. I asked him many times if he felt tired. But he said no. He wanted to catch up on his work. He told me he felt fine."

"What happened this morning?" asked Clara.

"Oh! He couldn't get out of bed. Now he says his chest hurts much more than before, and I can hear that his coughing has gotten worse. I am afraid he has a fever, too," sighed Hestia. "Thank goodness you're here, Clara. That old man came for his cane and left before Jon was awake. Had I known this would happen, I would have had a few words with him instead of 'thank you!'" she said angrily.

"Now now, Hestia," said Clara. "The wizards' medicine may have fooled Jon's body into thinking it was well, but it was Jon who tricked himself into believing he didn't need rest." Clara smiled at Jon. He looked very unhappy. She touched his forehead and asked him questions about how he felt. Clara searched through her medicine bag for the proper herbs to give Jon. She looked down and noticed that Melissa's picking basket bulged under its cloth cover.

"What do you have there, Melissa?" Clara asked.

"Blossoms from Elda-Mor, Mother."

"How wonderful!" Clara said. "We'll add them to Jon's tea."

Melissa was proud to be a part of Jon's healing. He looked so tired and sad that Melissa didn't know what to say to him. So she went with Clara and Hestia into the kitchen. Melissa knew her mother would take charge here.

"Hestia, start the water for the tea," Clara ordered. "Melissa, chop up this garlic bulb and this onion into tiny pieces. We'll start a poultice while the water is warming.

"Come, Hestia. I will show you how to make the poultice for Jon. You need to apply it twice a day, once on his chest, once on his back. It will draw the poisons out of his lungs." While she was speaking, she set a frying pan over the fire. She added a little oil to the pan and said, "Melissa, bring me the garlic and onions now." She cooked them until they were softened, then removed the pan from the fire.

"Now, Hestia, add a little thyme. Good! Now add vinegar and meal until you have a thick paste." She laid out a thin cloth and put the onion paste in the center. "Spread this out until it is a finger-width thick, like this. Then fold in the edges of the cloth until you have a nice flat package." After she finished making the poultice, Clara carried it to Jon's room and Melissa and Hestia followed. She helped Jon take off his nightshirt and asked him to lie perfectly still. She placed the wrapped poultice on his chest, rubbing her hands over it to make a smooth seal. Melissa knew this seal was important for the drawing power of the poultice. Then Clara covered Jon's entire chest with a small blanket and pulled the rest of his covers up to his chin.

"Now, Jon, move as little as you can until the poultice cools."

CLARA'S BALM FOR RASHES

(See page 75-77 for instructions on making oils and salves.)

In olive oil infuse:
1 part usnea
1/2 part nettle
1/2 part plantain
1/2 part calendula
1/2 part chamomile
1/4 part sage
1/4 part rosemary
1/4 part thyme

Strain off liquid. Heat 1 cup of the infused oil with 1 cup of almond or apricot kernel oil. Add 2-1/2 ounces of melted beeswax. Stir well and pour immediately into the containers. Allow the balm to cool completely before putting the lids on the containers.

Use liberally on cuts, scrapes, and scratches. Also good for chapped lips!

"Yes, ma'am," said Jon weakly. "The warmth feels so good."

"We'll leave you to rest now," Clara said softly. As they walked back to the kitchen, Clara told Hestia, "When the poultice becomes cold, take it off and throw it away. Then have Jon drink the tea. Do the poultice again tomorrow in the morning and in the evening. Have him drink the tea all day. I will come back the day after tomorrow."

"A thousand thanks and blessings to you, Clara," said Hestia, "and to you, too, Melissa. Would you like a ride home? Thor will be back soon with the horse and wagon."

"Thank you, Hestia. It's such a pretty day that I think we'll walk. We have plenty of time before dark."

As they headed out the door, they heard a soft rumbling sound. Melissa looked down the road to see if there were any wild pigs grunting about.

"Oh, what a sweet sound!" cried Hestia. "Jon is snoring. He is finally getting a restful sleep."

She waved goodbye to them. Clara and Melissa could not help but giggle as they went down the road.

Melissa was excited as they walked home. The herbs did work! But she didn't completely understand why. "Mother, why did the wizards' medicine go bad?" she asked.

"As far as I can tell, the wizards do not understand patience. They want healing to come quickly. Everything in nature takes its own time. A seed becomes a flower in its own time. A human seed grows to a baby in its mother's womb. Often, the most important part of healing is rest. When we are still, we can hear our inner voice, the truest part of ourselves. If we don't take time to be quiet and listen to that part of ourselves, our body makes us stop. We get sick, we stop, we listen. Then we heal our body and our spirit."

"Really, Mother?"

"Well, that is what I believe," Clara smiled. "But no matter why we are sick, we must heal in our own time. The herbs know that. They offer support and assistance for the return to health. Somehow, the wizards' medicine covers up how sick a person is. The person feels better before he is better. I don't quite understand it," Clara sighed. "I can't imagine how medicine that hurries the illness could be good for a person."

"I can't either, Mother," said Melissa.

"One thing you must know, Melissa," said Clara solemnly, "is that wizards' medicine, and even herbal medicine, is not the most important tool of healing. The best tools we have are warm hands for holding, ears willing to listen, and an open and loving heart."

"I understand," said Melissa.

Clara and Melissa walked on quietly for awhile. Then Melissa remembered the elder flowers in her basket. The rest of the way home, she shared with her mother the story of meeting Elda-Mor.

In June, Melissa went with Clara to gather dandelion leaves and flowers.

They had gone to a meadow at the edge of the forest to pick them. These dandelions looked different from the little ones that poked up from cracks in the cobblestone streets of the village. These dandelions grew in rich soil, and they hadn't been trampled by horses and humans like the poor dandelions in the village. The meadow dandelions had big pom-poms of a rich golden color.

"Mother, why do the dandelions keep growing in the village streets, if they know they will never be used?" asked Melissa.

"Plants that are very nutritious and can be used in abundance as food like to grow near us. They want us to see them so we won't forget them. So, although we no longer pick the dandelions in the village streets, they gently remind us to go to the meadows to harvest their brothers and sisters."

Clara and Melissa gathered the dandelion leaves for their dinner. They would chop them into small pieces for their salad or steam them like spinach. They also gathered flowers that could be eaten. Melissa loved to eat them after her mother cooked them in butter and sprinkled them with a little thyme.

Not all the flowers were for food, though. Clara would keep some separate to make into a healing oil. She would put the blossoms in a crock in the sun for two weeks. Then she would strain the flowers out of the oil. This potion was used to massage sore muscles. The golden glow of the flowers, plus the energy of the sun, brought healing energy to the body.

When Melissa and Clara had gathered enough flowers, they gave thanks to the dandelions for their gifts. They found some flowers that had already gone to seed and looked like little round puffballs. They picked them and, taking deep breaths, blew the delicate balls apart and let the wind scatter the seeds. In this way, they were planting more dandelions, replacing what they had taken.

In the summer, Melissa spent some time each day in the garden. She loved to visit with the calendulas because their spirits were the liveliest in the garden. Their colorful dressings of oranges, yellows, and golds called to her as she walked down the paths.

"Look at me. Look at me! Aren't we pretty?" the calendulas seemed to shout. Melissa often picked them to brighten up the kitchen table. They didn't mind. Plants don't mind being picked when they know it is for a purpose. They like to be made into food or medicine, or to be admired in a flower vase.

Once when Melissa was gathering the flowers, they spoke to her.

"You know, I'm not just another pretty face," said one yellow flower.

"Oh!" Melissa was a little startled.

THYME STEAM

Pick a handful of fresh thyme, or use about 1/4 cup dried thyme.

Place in a medium size bowl (glass or stainless steel). Pour boiling hot water over the thyme.

Bend over the bowl and put a towel over your head and the bowl to make a tent. Breathe deeply and enjoy! Stay under for as long as you can (5 to 15 minutes).

Keep hankies nearby as steaming can unblock the respiratory passages.

For more information on steams in general, see page 75.

Caution:
Don't put your face too close to the water. Steam from the boiling water can cause a burn.

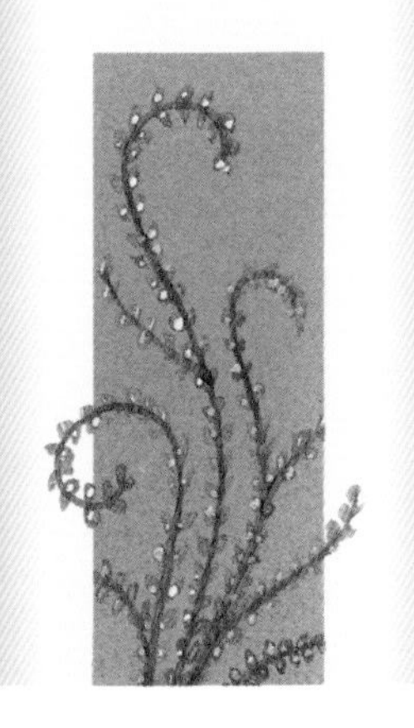

"Yes," an orange flower nodded in the sun, "it's time you learned a little more about us."

"Why, I'd be most happy to," said Melissa as she sat down beside them. She noticed their voices were low and deep. She remembered that her mother had given her tea of calendula last winter, and it had tasted deep, like the flowers sounded.

"First, we are very good to drink in the autumn and winter. We can keep you from getting colds and flus. We are very happy to protect you in this way."

"Our tea is also good for stomach problems," piped up a yellow flower.

"We're very good for the skin," started another. "We can make your skin glow as we do. If you have a sore that won't heal, we'll help it. You can drink our tea or wash with our waters. Sometimes humans and animals get itchy skin. Sometimes they get a fungus on their fingers or toes. A tea or a bath with us will make that go away."

"Don't forget the salve!" squeaked a baby calendula. Its bud was just beginning to open.

"Ah, yes," said an older gold flower. "You can ask your mother to teach you how to make a healing salve with us. She will show you how to mix our flowers with oils and beeswax. Then you have something magical you can carry in a little jar in your bag. The salve can help heal stings, burns, and cuts. It will take the itchiness out of rashes, especially for babies."

"I have seen my mother give little jars of salve to women whose babies have very sore, red bottoms. Perhaps that salve was made of you!" said Melissa.

The calendula nodded their heads proudly.

Melissa thanked the flowers as she put them in her basket. Then she hurried inside to share with her mother what she had learned.

Late one summer afternoon, as the sun was just beginning to set on the garden, Melissa saw fairies running from the thyme beds. She walked over to sit with the Grandfather Thyme plant.

"Grandfather, what were all the fairies doing in your branches?" asked Melissa.

"Why, this is where they live!" Grandfather Thyme answered in his old, slow voice.

"Oh, my!" said Melissa.

"In the evening," he continued, "the fairies like to fly from plant to plant, visiting all the flowers. Sometimes they go to dances in the forest. But during the day, they like to rest in my shade. They love the bees, and the bees love me. So when the bees come to gather sweet nectar from my flowers, it gives the bees and the fairies a chance to talk and catch up with each other."

"My mother says the honey from your flowers is very good medicine," said Melissa.

"That's because I am good medicine, and I give some of that to the bees in my nectar."

"Last year, when many of the children had colds, mother came to school with some of your branches. We boiled a pot of water on the wood stove, then placed your branches in it. At first, we all stood around the pot and breathed deeply. Later we went back to our schoolwork, but we kept adding fresh thyme to the water. We all felt better, and the classroom smelled so good! It also made me very hungry."

"Clara does pick a lot of me for cooking, so I'm not surprised. I would bet my smell reminds you of her stews and her casseroles. I'm sure you hurried home for supper that day!"

"Just sitting beside you now, smelling you, makes me hungry again. I think it's time to go in now," said Melissa.

"Good night. We will talk again, child. Remember, when you gather my branches, be careful not to disturb the bees or the fairies!"

Within the mighty stone walls of the great castle in the Capital sat Frederick, the Duke of Allopathy. The Duke was a man far removed from the people he was to protect. He had allowed himself to be caught in the web woven by a spider named Greed. He sat in his chambers in a comfortable chair by the hearth. No matter how close he was to the fire, though, it could never warm the coldness in his heart. When an old man in a gray cloak arrived, the Duke neither turned to greet him nor offered him a chair. He simply said, "Hemlock, what news?"

"Your Excellency, I have traveled to many villages in the Southland. I have spread word of the new medicines in clever, subtle ways. However, I am afraid there will be some resistance. Many of these ignorant people hang on to their old traditions," said Hemlock.

The Duke spoke in a voice choked with anger. "Resistance! I have spent too much time and money on this plan to accept resistance! This is to be my greatest undertaking. Being the sole supplier of medicine will give me the control I want over the kingdom, and it will fill my coffers, too!"

"Your Excellency, I believe I have a plan that will work," said Hemlock.

"Speak!" said the Duke.

"Your cousin, the King, has a weakness for the welfare of his people. If you can convince him their superstitions are harmful to them, if you can persuade him that the new medicine is for their benefit, then we can have our way. The King must proclaim a new law that allows no medicine but the King's medicine. If you can convince him that such a law is for the good of his people, your plan will be complete," said Hemlock.

"How can I be sure this will work?" said the Duke.

"Flatter the King. Tell him you realize how terribly busy he is with the affairs of state. Tell him you hate to trouble him with such unimportant matters. Then say that, for the sake of the people, you would be willing to take this task into your own hands."

The Duke smiled. "Hemlock, you are very clever and almost as wicked as I am.

When the plan is completed, you and your fellow wizards will be rewarded."

"Thank you, Your Excellency," said Hemlock.

"As soon as the ink on the new law is dry, I will take action," said the Duke. "I shall set out with my soldiers to see that the new order is well received." His eyes gleamed. "The King will be touched by my personal interest, and that will endear me to him even more. Hah!" The Duke laughed and Hemlock laughed—wicked laughter that sent shivers through the earth.

"You may go now, Hemlock," said the Duke.

"As you wish, Your Excellency," said Hemlock.

"But don't go far," said the Duke. "I will need you later. You must return to the villages after my journey—in secret, of course. Let no one see you. You must watch to see that everyone follows my command. And you must return to tell me if anyone disobeys."

"Very good, Your Excellency," the old wizard said as he departed.

The Duke called for his servant. "Send notice to the King's messenger that I wish to have an audience with His Majesty in the morning," said the Duke. "And bring me the finest wine from the cellars. I feel like celebrating."

"Yes, Your Excellency," said the servant as he bowed low.

The Duke sat comfortably in his chair and waited.

Melissa and Clara were working in the garden when they felt the ground

SPRING TONIC TEA

Mix together these dried herbs:
1/2 ounce dandelion leaf
1/2 ounce nettle
1/2 ounce red clover
1/2 ounce mint
1/2 ounce oat straw
1/2 ounce calendula flowers or rose petals

Using 1 teaspoon of the herbal combination for each 1 cup of water, pour boiling water over the herbs. Cover and allow to steep for 20 minutes. Strain off the liquid. Grape or apple juice may be added as a sweetener.

Suggested use:
Drink 1 or 2 cups daily as a beverage tea during February, March, and April. Drink for 4 or 5 days a week. For children under 10, dilute by half with water or juice.

rumble. They rushed to the roadside just as a regiment of soldiers rode by. They couldn't see who rode in front, but Melissa thought she recognized one of the banners a rider carried. The red and black flag with the gold dragon belonged to Frederick, the Duke of Allopathy. Melissa and Clara waited for the dust to settle and started down the road to the village.

Sure enough, when Melissa and Clara arrived at the village courtyard, they saw the Duke of Allopathy. Melissa stood close to her mother as she watched him. Everything about him was different from the villagers. For one thing, he didn't seem healthy when compared to the people of Yarrow. His skin was pale against the fine dark cloth he wore. His face and body were pointed and sharp, not at all like the roundness of the villagers. If the people of her village were all plump, warm, freshly baked loaves of bread, Melissa thought, this man would be the stale, moldy loaf forgotten on the back porch. Even his smile was different. It came from his lips, but not from his eyes. She noticed he was not tender with his horse or friendly to his men.

The soldiers moved the gathering crowd outside of the circle they had cleared for the Duke. They set a platform for Frederick, the Duke of Allopathy, to stand on. He took a scroll from his pouch, unrolled the parchment, and decreed: "From this day forward, the medicine of the wizards of the Capital shall be the medicines of the kingdom. These and only these medicines may be used. They may not be obtained through trade but must be purchased with gold on festival days. The King's wizards have spent much time and much money to make these medicines. It is the King's desire to keep his kingdom healthy and to protect his people from the superstitions of the old witch ways. Those caught using plants and witches' potions will be taken to the Capital dungeon. So say I, Frederick, the Duke of Allopathy, spokesman for the King. Long live the King!"

And the villagers shouted, "Long live the King!"

They did not gossip and chatter as they left the courtyard. They were silent and hung their heads as if looking for something they lost on the ground. They were really looking into their own hearts.

As the crowd began to leave, a nervous horse suddenly reared up and spilled its rider with a loud clang of armor. Another soldier rushed to the side of the fallen knight and removed his helmet. His face was clenched with pain.

The townspeople were curious but did not want to linger near the Duke and his men. Melissa and Clara watched from behind a nearby tree. The helpful knight rushed to the Duke and cried, "Your Excellency, Basil has fallen and cannot be moved."

"Then I suppose he is doomed to stay in this quaint little town," sneered the Duke.

"Your Excellency, he may need only an hour of rest."

"We cannot wait for one soldier," shouted the Duke. "I want to be done with the next village before sundown."

"Sire, perhaps I can stay with him awhile. We can catch up with you tomorrow."

"Chiron, stay or go! I have no care. But remember, you will lose your wages for every day you do not ride with us." And with that, Frederick, the Duke of Allopathy, galloped away.

When the Duke was out of sight, Clara and Melissa moved closer to the two soldiers left behind. They watched as Chiron tried to help his friend Basil get out of his heavy armor.

"Be careful, friend," moaned Basil. "The slightest movement gives me pain. I fear I am hurt so badly I shall never mend."

Clara boldly approached the soldier and said, "If you are willing, the plants can help you mend."

"Oh, m' lady, yes. Please help me!" cried Basil.

"We must get you inside," Clara said. "Where you can lie down."

"I fear I can't go far, m' lady," said Basil.

Clara looked around. The nearest house was that of her friend Laurel. Laurel stood in her doorway. She, too, had been watching the soldiers. She admired the way Chiron had stayed with his friend. She saw gentleness and concern in his face. She did not think such a kind person would be one of the Duke's soldiers. Laurel walked over to the fallen soldier and helped Melissa, Clara, and Chiron carry Basil into her home.

Clara sent Melissa home to bring back chamomile flowers, fresh comfrey leaves, and oil of St. John's wort. Only for a second did Melissa remember that she was defying the King's new order. The wounded soldier's need, and the love and respect she felt for her mother, pushed all other thoughts aside.

As Melissa gathered the comfrey leaves, she remembered her mother's words: "Comfrey comforts everything it touches." Melissa knew that comfrey made into tea soothes the lungs and the stomach. Drinking it also makes the bones strong. Clara often used it as food, saying it is full of vitamins and minerals. A salve made of the root of the leaves was very soothing for cuts and rashes. Melissa knew that today Clara would use the comfrey leaves as a poultice for the soldier's painful back. Comfrey poultices speed the healing of bumps, sprains, and even broken bones. That's why in the Treasure Book Melissa's grandmother called comfrey "knit-bone."

When she returned, Melissa helped Clara make tea of chamomile and comfrey for Basil to drink. They rubbed the oil of St. John's wort on Basil's painful back. After the oil had soaked in, they placed a poultice of bruised comfrey leaves on it.

Then Clara taught Melissa, Chiron, and Laurel a gentle

FALL TONIC TEA

Mix together these dried herbs:

1-1/2 ounces dandelion root
1/2 ounce marshmallow root
1/2 ounce orange peel
1/2 ounce ginger
1/2 ounce licorice root
1 ounce cinnamon (stick or chips)

Place the herbs in a saucepan with cold water, using 1 teaspoon per cup. Bring to simmer. Cover and allow to simmer for 20 minutes. Remove from heat and strain off the liquid. Juice or honey may be added for sweetener.

Suggested use:
Drink 1 or 2 cups daily as a beverage tea during August, September, and October. Drink for 4 or 5 days a week. For children under 10, dilute by half with water or juice.

healing song. They held hands in a circle around Basil to sing it to him. The song, Clara told them, would help his body remember what it was like to be strong, to be without pain. At first they sang awkwardly. But following Clara's clear lead, they sang it several times. The last round of the song was so incredible in its healing power that it seemed the angels had joined them.

They imagined Basil whole and well again. They sent him love and healing from their hearts. Then Laurel covered him well with blankets, and they left him to rest.

"I think he's going to be just fine, don't you, Clara?" chirped Laurel, who was one of the village weavers. She was known for her cheerful, generous spirit. She liked to make merry tunes as she wove her threads in and out the loom. Later she taught her songs to the schoolchildren. She lived alone and spent so many hours singing and weaving that she never had enough time to look after her house. Pieces of wood hung loose here and there.

"I do think he'll mend well. He's young and strong," replied Clara. "I will check on him tomorrow. But will you be all right, Laurel?" She eyed Chiron cautiously.

"Oh, I don't mind having some company. Since the soldier will take some time to mend, I might get some work out of this one." She laughed and patted Chiron on the shoulder. "There is plenty around here that needs fixing."

"I would be honored to help you, m' lady," said Chiron.

"Tell us, Chiron," said Laurel, "how did you come to be in service of the Duke?"

"Oh, I believe it's just one of those things that happened to me," Chiron sighed. "Basil and I grew up together in a small town in the Northland. Some years back,

we decided we wanted to see the world. We had many great adventures, but we also got into a bit of trouble for hunting on the Duke's land. When he saw we were strong and somewhat skilled in fighting, he gave us a choice. We could go to jail, where we would likely die of some horrid disease, or we could join his guard. So here we are."

"That's quite a story," said Clara.

"Yes. I'm sorry Basil is hurt, but perhaps being in this little village for a while will be the best adventure of all," said Chiron as he looked at Laurel.

"My mother used to say," said Laurel, "If you wait a while after something bad happens, you'll see that it was really for the best."

For the next two weeks, Clara and Melissa visited Laurel's house to care for Basil. They gave him comfrey and nettle tea to make his bones and muscles strong. They continued to rub his back with oil of St. John's wort and apply comfrey leaves to it. Soon he was doing gentle stretching exercises they taught him. When he felt well enough to walk, he strolled the village and carried news from shop to shop.

A season passed. In the mornings, Melissa gathered herbs for her mother before school. Clara was busy preparing the garden for winter. Melissa's friend Jon worked hard at his father's forge. Chiron stayed on with Laurel. Not only did he repair her house, but he built a large weaving room for her. Laurel herself was building the larger loom of her dreams to go inside the new room. Basil apprenticed with the town bakers who had no children of their own to teach. He

YARROW GARGLE FOR SORE THROATS

Mix these dried herbs together:
1/4 ounce yarrow
1/4 ounce sage
1/4 ounce comfrey leaf

Using 1 teaspoon of the herbal mixture per cup, pour boiling water over dried herbs. Cover and allow to steep for 15 minutes. Strain off the liquid and let cool to body temperature. Gargle as needed. Refrigerate the unused portion.

still strolled the village every day to hear and spread news from shop to shop.

One chilly autumn day, Clara asked Melissa to go to the forest to gather the herb the town was named for, yarrow.

Yarrow stood tall like a soldier in the forest. Melissa recognized him right away, his white blossoms atop his tall stalk like a fancy admiral's hat. When she drew near with her gathering basket, he spoke to her in his precise voice. It reminded her of the times the mayor spoke at village gatherings.

"Girl," he said, "what do you want here?"

"If it pleases you, Sir Yarrow, I am here to gather your flowers for my mother's medicine chest. I have brought crystals and prayers as an offering."

"Well I have graced many a medicine cabinet, I tell you. I have been a healer since ancient times. I have healed many a wound in the battlefield. Most especially, I was used by a very famous Greek warrior named Achilles. He used me to stop the bleeding and heal the cuts of his soldiers. His mother knew my powers, too. So strongly did she believe in my power to protect that she held Achilles by the ankle and dipped him in a tub of my waters when he was just a baby. Alas, his ankle did not receive any of my healing water and was always to be his weak spot. It was upon his heel that he was mortally wounded."

Melissa believed Yarrow was strong. Otherwise, how could he talk so much without stopping? Just as Melissa was thinking this, Yarrow started talking again.

"I have other uses, too. You will have to visit me many times to hear them all. Since the winter chill is coming, I will tell you I am very good for fevers. I could, of course, do the job all by myself, but some herbalists like to mix me with elder and peppermint for flus and colds."

"Yarrow, I know now that you are a very worthy herb," said Melissa, as formally as she could. "I hope to learn all I can about you. This time, with your permission, I must pick what I can and go. I have brought you these crystals to thank you for your healing gifts. The sun is starting to go down behind the trees, and I must get home before dark."

"Ah, yes, everyone is in a hurry nowadays. Go ahead, and be sure to pick the choicest blossoms and leaves. You'll make the finest medicines from me. By the way, thank you for the crystals. They'll be a lovely addition to my forest floor."

Melissa picked the flowers, thanked the yarrow, and headed home. Tired, she knew why her mother asked her to gather yarrow today.

As it was fall, Clara and Melissa soon returned to the dandelion meadow. The flowers were gone, and any leaves that were left were shriveled and turning brown. This was the time to harvest their roots.

They dug deep, where the roots had journeyed into the earth, to bring up health-giving minerals. "Eating the root of this plant, or drinking a tea made of it, is important to staying healthy, Melissa," Clara told her.

"Why is that, Mother?"

"It helps our livers stay strong. The liver is a part of our body that does many amazing things. It helps us to process our foods and takes poisons out of our bodies. Many of the problems I see are caused by weak livers."

When they had filled their baskets with roots, they got ready to leave. They made sure to fill all the holes they had dug with dirt and to cover them again with fallen leaves. They gave thanks for their harvest and left a small crystal as a gift for the Earth Mother.

"Mother, whenever we dig in the forest or garden, I feel very strong and whole in my body," said Melissa.

"That is because our digging brings out that solid earth."

"I don't understand," said Melissa.

"All the elements—earth, air, fire, water, and metal—are a part of us," explained Clara. "When we work with an element, it helps us to connect with that part of ourselves. Earth, our body. Fire, our spirit and our emotions. Water, our blood and our feelings. Air, our breath. Metal, our will.

"Look at Jon's father," she continued, "He works with metal and fire all day long. He is very strong and spirited. Fishermen work in the water of the earth and have learned its rhythms. They know how to flow with the tide. The message bearers who run from town to town learn the secrets of the air. Their lungs grow strong, and they learn that life is breath. As herbalists, we work mostly with the earth. It is good to seek balance with all the elements. Can you see how that might be done?"

Melissa thought for a while and said, "When I make a cup of tea, I do that! I blow on the fire to get it started, to heat the water in the pot, to put the herbs in, to drink and heal."

"You're very clever," said her mother. "I think you'll be a very good herbalist."

As they neared home, Melissa began to feel uncomfortable. It was the same strange feeling she had when she met Hemlock in the meadow.

She whispered, "Mother—"

Clara put her finger to her lips. Melissa understood that she felt it, too.

They took another step. Then Clara stopped. She gathered her strength in a deep breath and said, "Who's there?" She waited, but there was no answer. "Come out," she said. "Are you in trouble? Are you hurt? We can help you." Still there was silence.

Clara put her arm around Melissa. "Whatever it is, it doesn't seem to wish us harm, nor does it want to reveal itself. Let's go home, but keep your eyes and ears sharp along the way."

They went along the meadow trail and did not see the old

man in a gray cloak who hid in the forest trees beyond.

Hemlock returned to the Capital and entered the great stone walls of the castle. He again found the Duke seated by the fireplace, staring into the fire.

"What news, Hemlock?" he said.

"Your Excellency, in most villages everything is going according to your plan. I—"

"Most villages!" the Duke interrupted. "What do you mean?"

Hemlock hesitated. "Well, Your Excellency, in some villages live families that have been herbal healers for generations. The poor villagers are convinced the herbalists are important to their town. They are not ready to give up the old ways."

"Not ready!" shouted the Duke. He stood quickly and faced Hemlock. "We will make them ready! My men know how to bring them to reason."

"Yes, Your Excellency," said Hemlock calmly.

The Duke sat back in his chair. "The time is not right for this now," he said. "The weather is changing, and soon all the roads will be covered with snow."

"Your Excellency," said Hemlock. "There is no hurry. Spring will come soon enough. Then the uncooperative towns can be dealt with."

"Yes. Wise counsel, Hemlock. The winter season will also give the wizards plenty of time to increase our supply of medicine. Go now, and tell them we will have a prosperous spring. Hah!"

"Yes, Your Excellency," said Hemlock, and he bowed and left the room.

The Duke went back to staring at the fire.

Melissa and Clara lived in harmony with the seasons. They ate the foods and herbs of each season and planted their garden according to the cycles of the moon. In the summer, they would get up at dawn with the rooster's crow. In the winter, they would go to bed early, not long after dark.

As much as Melissa loved the long, warm days of summer filled with swimming, gardening, and playing with her friends, she loved the winter too.

Winter was a cozy time for reading the Treasure Book by the fireplace or listening to Clara and her women friends tell stories. It was a time of mending and sorting. It was a time of baking. It was a time of peppermint.

Melissa could not imagine the winter holidays without peppermint. When she and her mother would go visiting, they would always take freshly baked peppermint cookies. Melissa would help her mother mix the dough. Then Clara would roll it out and let Melissa choose what shapes to cut.

PEPPERMINT COOKIES

Ingredients:
1 cup butter
1 cup honey
3 eggs
1 teaspoon vanilla extract
1 teaspoon cream of tartar
1 teaspoon baking soda
1 cup dried peppermint leaf
3-4 cups flour

In a mixing bowl, blend the butter and honey together until creamy. Add eggs and vanilla, mixing thoroughly. Mix in the baking soda and peppermint leaf. Gradually add the flour until the dough is smooth and elastic.

Form into a ball, cover and chill for 30 minutes.

Preheat oven to 350 degrees.

Using a floured surface, roll the cookie dough out to approximately 1/4 inch. Cut it into shapes with cookie cutters.

Bake 7 to 10 minutes or until edges are slightly brown.

They would sing together as stars, moons, and heart shapes baked in the oven. Sometimes, they used spices or raisins to decorate them. They always tasted the first ones out of the oven, just to make sure they turned out right.

Winter was a time for feasting. It seemed as though almost every villager took a turn at having a gathering. Sometimes, Melissa ate too much and had a tummy ache. At these times, peppermint was a true friend. Her mother would make her a cup of peppermint tea and in no time at all she would feel better again.

Sometimes, if Melissa felt a cold coming on, Clara would give her a bath with peppermint and thyme and bundle her off to bed. There she would give Melissa a tea of chamomile, peppermint, lemon, and honey to drink as she read her a bedtime story. Melissa always felt better the next day.

It was on such a night that Melissa learned about the plant she was named after. She was having trouble getting to sleep when Clara brought her a cup of lemon balm tea.

"Mother, this is my favorite tea," said Melissa.

"I am glad, because lemon balm will always be very special to me and to you."

"Why is that, Mother?"

"Because each herb can have two or more names. The other name for lemon balm is melissa. That is where your name came from. When you were inside me waiting to be born, I often sat by the lemon balm plant. Its fragrance soothed me. I would cut it to spread around the house to make it smell good, and I would drink it as my nighttime tea. It was such a pleasure and comfort to me, as I knew you would be, that I decided to honor you with its name."

"I think it is a good plant to be named after, Mother. Thank you. But why is lemon balm also called melissa?"

"In ancient language, *melissa* means bees. Bees like lemon balm so much that people sometimes called it bee-leaf. Beekeepers rub their hives with lemon balm leaves to keep their bees happy, so they'll want to stay at those hives."

"Why do you use lemon balm?" asked Melissa sleepily.

"It is one of my favorite herbs for young children. It is very good for tummy aches and flus and colds. It is good for the skin, and I like to bathe in it. It can be a very calming tea, but it can also bring merriment. If I am ever feeling sad, I like to drink a tea of lemon balm mixed with lavender. It always makes me feel better. I think it's helpful for sleep, don't you?" But Melissa did not answer. Her eyes were closed and she was fast asleep.

Winter turned to spring. Along the paths of the forest lay a thick carpet of green clover. It was cool and comfortable to lie down in or to walk through with bare feet. Little red blossoms poked up out of the carpet on slender stems. When the wind blew, they danced like delicate ballerinas. When Melissa lay down on the ground beside them, she could hear them softly sing.

The song lulled Melissa to sleep, but she could still hear it as she dreamed. Her dream took her to an ancient meadow in an ancient land. She saw shepherds with their flocks of sheep. She saw the dried, dying blossoms of clover cling to the sheep's curly wool to travel with them to new meadows. The seeds from the blossoms fell to the new soil to sprout and grow. New clovers blossomed, and once again ballerinas danced on the carpet of green.

Then Melissa dreamed of young maidens with sturdy hands picking the flowers. They placed the red blossoms in baskets woven by their grandmothers. They hung the baskets in the breezy porches of their homes so the flowers would dry. Preserved this way, the flowers would be placed in earthen jars beside other herbs in the grandmothers' healing cabinets. From the grandmothers, Melissa had learned the power of red clover and how to make medicine with it. She had watched them wash babies with it to help their rashes. She watched them give its tea to those with itchy red skin. The grandmothers had told her this herb was also good for coughs and colds. It comes up in the spring, they had said, bringing up all the strength gathered by the earth during the winter. Drinking the tea will give that strength to you, the grandmothers had told her.

The trees cast a shadow, and the clover stopped singing. Melissa awakened and rose to head dreamily home.

CHILDREN'S NIGHTTIME TEA

1 ounce lemon balm
1 ounce chamomile
1/2 ounce lavender
1/2 ounce mint
1/2 ounce rose petals

Using 1 teaspoon of the herbal combination for each 1 cup of water, pour boiling water over the herbs.

Cover and allow to steep for 15 to 20 minutes. Strain off the liquid. Honey (honey for children 3 and over only) or apple juice may be added as a sweetener.

Dilute by half with water or juice for children under 5.

As Melissa walked through the door, she saw that her mother had set the table with two teacups and a plate of cookies. Clara was just putting a teapot on the table. Melissa lifted the lid of the teapot. Inside, red blossoms floated in the water.

"Oh, Mother!" cried Melissa. "How did you know?"

"At this time of year, when I was your age, I heard the song of the clovers, too," Clara said.

They both smiled.

As May neared, Melissa was sent daily to a certain part of the forest to visit an old hawthorn tree. As soon as his white blossoms were completely open, she was supposed to run to the village to let the people know it was time for the May Day festivities to begin. The leaves and flowers would decorate the town and its people. There would be much feasting, singing, and merrymaking. The mayor would become the fool, bakers would become jugglers, and farmers would become actors performing for the town. It would be three days and three nights of joyful celebration!

On one of her visits to the hawthorn, Melissa felt a strong urge to hug his trunk and stroke his branches. She had to be careful because part of Hawthorn's name comes from the little thorns he bears between his leaves. As she stroked the tree, she heard a low, rough voice come from deep within its bark.

"Why, thank you, Melissa. It feels ever so good to know I am loved."

"You are loved, Hawthorn. Don't you know that? The townspeople wait excitedly

each year to see your lovely white flowers. That is why I am here."

"Ah, it must be nearing May Day. Sometimes, I find it hard to rouse from winter's sleep. Yet my sap is running strong, my leaves are green and shiny, and I do believe my buds will open any day now."

"And after your buds come your flowers, and after the flowers come your delicious berries," said Melissa. She smiled as she thought of the tasty jam her mother made from them.

"Do you know the healing gift within my berries, Melissa?" asked Hawthorn.

"No, I haven't learned that yet, dear tree."

"Well, then, I shall tell you. They are the very best thing you can eat for your heart. For those with hearts that are weak, I make them strong. For those with hearts that run too fast, I help them relax. For those with healthy hearts, I keep them healthy," said the tree.

He bent his branches to lean close to Melissa, as if to share a special secret. "It is important to keep your heart strong because that is where your best decisions are made. If you bring your life's questions to your heart for answers, you will never go wrong.

"Hearts don't have it easy," the tree continued. "When we are sad or when we are worried or disappointed, our hearts carry the weight. My berries, plus love and laughter, give our hearts the strength to carry on."

"My heart feels good just sitting with you, Hawthorn," said Melissa. She thought she could feel the tree smile.

"Thank you, Melissa. Now it is time for you to run along home. Visit me again tomorrow, and I may have some flowers blooming for you and for your village, too!"

On her way home from the Hawthorn tree, Melissa heard loud noises from the courtyard. As she neared it, she saw Frederick, the Duke of Allopathy, and his men. They looked more fierce than ever. Wasting no time, the soldiers rounded up the townspeople to hear the words the Duke had brought to them.

The Duke stood in the center of the courtyard. He was dressed in layers of red and black cloth, and around his neck he wore a large gold necklace with the King's emblem. Wearing the symbol of the rose and the lion meant he had the right to speak for the King and take what actions he felt necessary. He looked very powerful and very wicked. He shouted his words with an angry voice.

"People of Yarrow! It has come to the King's attention that a witch in this town continues to defy His Majesty's orders. She is not only breaking the law but forcing you to break the law along with her! The making and giving of medicine from plants is not allowed. Bring this witch to me or beware! I wear the emblem of the King and shall use any means to enforce his law. I shall refresh myself at

HEALTHY HEART DELIGHT

1-1/2 ounce hawthorn berries
1/2 ounce borage
1/2 ounce ginko

Put 1-1/2 ounces hawthorn berries in 2 quarts of water and bring to a simmer. Cover and allow to simmer for 15 minutes. Add 1/2 ounce borage and 1/2 ounce ginko.

Cover and remove from the heat and let steep for 10 minutes. Strain off the liquid.

Add an equal part of raspberry or cranberry juice and stir. Serve hot or cold.

your tavern. I expect the witch to be brought to me before my meal is finished. That is all. Long live the King!"

And the people shouted, "Long live the King!" But not very loudly.

Melissa was so scared, her knees felt weak, but she ran home as fast as she could. When she told her mother what the Duke had said, Clara sighed and shook her head.

"You must be brave now, my little one, for I must go to the King. Who knows what the Duke will do to Yarrow and its people if I do not go? It would not be fair to those who have trusted us for so long."

Melissa and her mother held each other and cried. Clara packed a small bag for herself. She got down the Treasure Book and told Melissa to hide it and keep it safe. It was her book now.

Just then, they heard noises outside their little home. Looking out the window, they saw the villagers gathering in a circle around the house. Each person stood firmly, hands clasping the next person's. They formed a human chain. At the center of the circle, standing at their front door, were Chiron, Jon, Basil, and Laurel. Chiron and Basil held their swords, while Laurel and Jon had pitchforks.

Soon Frederick, the Duke of Allopathy, and his soldiers arrived. They had become suspicious when the town became quiet and followed the trail to Clara's house. The Duke laughed when he saw the townsfolk surrounding the home.

"Oh, stupid, stupid people," the Duke sneered. "Do you think you can keep out my men? These fierce soldiers have done battle with armies ten times stronger

SALVE FOR ITCHY CONDITIONS

(See general information on salve and oil making on page 75-77.)

In olive oil, infuse:
1 part red clover
1 part plantain
1 part chickweed
1 part yarrow
1 part lavender
1 part comfrey leaf

Strain. Heat 1 cup of the infused oil with 1 cup of almond or apricot oil. To these 2 cups of heated oil, add 2-1/2 ounces of melted beeswax.

Stir well and pour into containers. Do not cover until completely cool. Use liberally on itchy, dry skin conditions.

than you. Soldiers, draw your swords," ordered the Duke.

And the soldiers did so. The gleam from the sun dancing off the shiny metal of their swords was blinding. It made these men in armor all the more terrifying, but the townspeople held their ground.

"For your defiance," shouted the Duke, "my men will take your witch and all your possessions as well. By order of the King—soldiers, attack!"

But the soldiers didn't move.

While the Duke spoke, the solders had been looking at the townspeople. The soldiers were used to fighting other soldiers for land or gold. They had never fought weaponless people who were trying to save a friend. They looked into the eyes of Basil and Chiron, men who had once been soldiers with them, who had ridden beside them and shared food with them. And when they looked into Basil's and Chiron's eyes, they saw into those two men's hearts. For each soldier, those eyes became a mirror that let them look deep into their own hearts.

The soldiers became ashamed. They knew they should not and could not hurt these villagers. These noble townspeople were trying to save a friend. They were saving a tradition that had kept them happy, healthy, and strong for generations.

The soldiers got off their horses and laid down their weapons.

Frederick, the Duke of Allopathy, was furious! His face turned ugly and red, and he shouted, "Fools, fools! I will have all your heads for this! The King shall hear of this. You have not seen the last of me." He reared up his horse and galloped away toward the Capital.

The townspeople and the soldiers laughed and cheered. Melissa and Clara came out of the house and hugged and thanked each person. The mayor declared a holiday, and everyone set off to prepare for a festival. The next day, Melissa and other young village girls went to the hawthorn tree to gather flowers. They brought them to the village courtyard to decorate it and themselves. The rest of the village brought food and drink and musical instruments to play. They sang and danced and feasted for three days and three nights.

The soldiers became a part of the town. They lent their strong backs to the toil in the fields, and Yarrow prospered. They gave their armor to Jon, and he used the metal to make tools.

Basil became a very good baker. He was known for his especially delicious herb breads, which he made using herbs from Clara's garden.

Chiron and Laurel had fallen in love. Their marriage gave the village good reason for another festival.

Clara continued to be the healer for Yarrow.

Frederick, the Duke of Allopathy, did not return to Yarrow. Just in case he might,

Melissa worked more than ever at her mother's side. She also spent more time with the plants. She wanted to learn the craft of an herbalist and be strong like her mother. She wanted to be able to preserve the old ways, no matter who or what might come to destroy them.

News of the Duke was heard now and then—how he traveled from town to town, threatening the old ways. Some villagers believed him. They gave up their traditions and lived in fear. But in the towns where the people had strong beliefs and hearts filled with love, it was as it had been in Yarrow. The villagers wondered: Why should the King bother the people who use herbs? The townspeople didn't mind if the King and his wizards in the Capital used their own medicines. But the villagers of Yarrow honored and cherished the plants, and the plants continued to offer their healing gifts.

So it was long ago, and so it is today.

GENERAL INSTRUCTIONS FOR HERB USAGE

HERB STEAMS

Herb steams are good for clearing congestion in the nose, sinuses, bronchia, and lungs. Breathing deeply while steaming gets the healing power of the herb where it's needed most.

Cosmetically, facial steams are great for cleansing and clearing complexions. While steaming, the pores of the skin are opened, releasing toxins. At the same time, the healing properties of the herb are discharged by the steam and absorbed by the skin. Ȧfter steaming, it is important to splash with cold water to close pores.

To steam:

In a glass or stainless steel bowl, place a small handful of herbs. Pour 1 to 2 quarts of boiling water over the herbs. Bend over the bowl and put a towel over you and the bowl. Don't get too far down over the bowl, as you don't want a steam burn. Breathe deeply and enjoy. Stay under as long as you can. You can come up from under the towel to take a short break if needed. If you are steaming for respiratory congestion, keep hankies nearby as steaming effectively unblocks the respiratory passages.

Suggested herbs for congestion and colds: thyme, oregano, mint, mullein, sage, and eucalyptus.

Suggested herbs for facial steams: rosemary, lavender, roses, elder flower, calendula, lemon balm, red clover, chamomile, violets, and yarrow.

INFUSED HERBAL OIL—DRY HERBS

In the top part of a double boiler, place about 2 cups of dried herbs. Cover with olive oil about 1 inch over the herbs. Heat the double boiler and stir often. You want the oil to heat, not to cook. If the flowers look fried, you've burned your oil and must start over. Do this for 1 to 2 hours. Take the telephone or a book with you into the kitchen (just don't leave the pot!) and keep on stirring. After cooking, remove from the heat and let cool. Strain through a cloth. Squeeze thoroughly to get all the good stuff out of the herb. Herbs can then be disposed of or placed in the compost. Store the oil in a completely dry glass jar (any water can make the oil go rancid) placed in a cool, dark cupboard.

Almost any herb can be infused into oil in this way. Make sure the herb is absolutely dry when you put it into the oil. You can make combination oils for specific purposes. As you learn more about herbs, you can make antifungal, burn, antiseptic, and other oils and salves.

INFUSED HERB OIL—FRESH HERBS

Collect the flowering tops of the plan when some of the buds are still closed. Chop and bruise these with a knife or in a blender. Fill a glass jar 3/4 full with the chopped herb. Pour olive oil over the herb and fill the jar. Screw the lid on tight. Place in a brown paper bag and put in the sun or a warm area for 2 or 3 weeks. Strain the oil and compost the herb. Keep the oil in a cool cupboard. Every week check for brown "dirt" to appear in the bottom of the jar. This is water from the plant, and it can make the oil go rancid. Pour off the oil into a fresh bottle, leaving the "dirt" behind. Do this until no more "dirt" appears. This oil is like gold in your medicine chest. Appreciate it. Use it.

Use this method of oil making whenever you want to use the herb fresh, such as dandelion flowers, violets, mullein flower, or St. John's wort.

HERB SALVE BALM

In a saucepan, heat the infused herbal oil you have made using a very low heat. You want to heat the oil just enough so the the beeswax doesn't harden in it. In the oven on low heat, your beeswax has been melting in a Pyrex measuring cup. Use 1-1/4 ounces melted beeswax per 1 cup herb oil. Add the beeswax to the heated oil and stir. I ladle the mixture into the warm Pyrex measuring cup for easy pouring into my containers. All the utensils (ladle, sauce pan, and measuring cup) must be warm, or the beeswax will harden on contact. Pour the oil and beeswax mix into your salve containers. Artichoke heart jars, pimento jars, and baby food jars are great for this. Make sure they are well washed and completely dry. After filling the jars, lay a piece of waxed paper over them so that nothing falls into them while they are cooling. Do not put the lids on until they are cool, or you'll get unwanted condensation.

If you are unhappy with the texture of your salve, you can add more or less beeswax: more if you like a solid salve, less if you want it softer. One way to test this before you pour the salve into the jars is to dip a spoon into the mixture and place the spoon into the freezer. Let it sit for a minute or so. It will cool and harden rapidly, and you'll get an idea of the texture of your salve. You can adjust it in the saucepan at this point by adding more oil or beeswax. Make pretty labels with stickers and give the extra jars to your friends.

STORAGE AND USE OF YOUR HERBS

Your herbs will stay fresher longer when stored in glass jars with lids. They also appreciate being kept out of the direct sunlight and away from excessive heat.

INFUSIONS AND DECOCTIONS

The traditional ways of making strong herbal teas are infusions and decoctions. Teas are easy and very effective methods of taking herbs for health and pleasure.

INFUSIONS GENERALLY ARE MADE FROM THE SOFTER PLANT PARTS, SUCH AS LEAVES, FLOWERS, AND STEMS.

For this method, use one teaspoon of dry herb for each cup of water. Pour the boiling water over the herb. Cover and steep for 10 to 15 minutes. (Chamomile and peppermint need to steep for only 5 minutes.)

DECOCTIONS ARE MADE FROM HARD PLANT MATERIALS SUCH AS ROOTS, BARK, AND SEEDS.

Place one teaspoon of dry herb for each cup of cold water. Bring this to a boil in a covered container. Allow to simmer at a low boil for 15 to 30 minutes. Strain and cool to desired temperature before drinking.

A traditional rule of thumb states that chronic problems require one teaspoon of herb per cup of water, while acute conditions call for one tablespoon of herb per cup of water in both infusions and decoctions.

Herb teas may be made in large quantities, such as 1 quart or 1 gallon, and may be served hot or iced. Teas made this way will last in the refrigerator 2 to 3 days.

OTHER HERBAL PREPARATIONS

In addition to teas, herbs can be ground and capsulated. This provides the convenience of capsules and the effectiveness of eating the whole herb. They also can be made into tinctures (alcohol extracts) or salves (for external use). Some excellent books on herb uses and preparations are *Herbal Healing for Women* by Rosemary Gladstar, *The New Holistic Herbal* by David Hoffman and *Herbs: Partners in Life* by Adele Dawson.

Dry Creek Herb Farm and Learning Center is located in the beautiful Sierra Foothills, northeast of Sacramento, California. If you plan on visiting the area and would like to receive a calendar of events, workshops, and apprenticeship programs, please send $1.00 to the address below.

Dry Creek Herb Farm also publishes a delightful mail order catalog of organic and wildcrafted herbs, herb products, natural skin care, and books. To receive a catalog, send $2.00 to:

Dry Creek Herb Farm and Learning Center
13935 Dry Creek Road
Auburn, California 95602
(916) 878-2441

If you would like to purchase additional copies of *The Herbalist of Yarrow,* check your local bookstore or call or write:

TZEDAKAH PUBLICATIONS
P.O. Box 221097
Sacramento, CA 95822
1-800-316-1824

N
Calamus River
Laurel's Home
TOWN SQUARE
Bakery
Jon's Home
Hawthorn Tree
School
MAP OF
YARROW